MS. MARVEL
ARMY OF ONE

PREVIOUSLY

After a strange Terrigen Mist descended upon Jersey City, Kamala Khan was imbued with polymorph powers. Using her new abilities to fight evil and protect Jersey City, she became the all-new Ms. Marvel!

MS. MARVEL: ARMY OF ONE. Contains material originally published in magazine form as MS. MARVEL (2015) #1-12. First printing 2020. ISBN 978-1-302-92363-1. Published by MARVEL WORLDWIDE, INC., a subsidiary of MARVEL ENTERTAINMENT, LLC. OFFICE OF PUBLICATION: 1290 Avenue of the Americas, New York, NY 10104. © 2020 MARVEL No similarity between any of the names, characters, persons, and/or institutions in this magazine with those of any living or dead person or institution is intended, and any such similarity which may exist is purely coincidental. **Printed in Canada.** KEVIN FEIGE, Chief Creative Officer; DAN BUCKLEY, President, Marvel Entertainment; JOE QUESADA, EVP & Creative Director; DAVID BOGART, Associate Publisher & SVP of Talent Affairs; TOM BREVOORT, VP, Executive Editor; NICK LOWE, Executive Editor, VP of Content, Digital Publishing; DAVID GABRIEL, VP of Print & Digital Publishing; JEFF YOUNGQUIST, VP of Production & Special Projects; ALEX MORALES, Director of Publishing Operations; DAN EDINGTON, Managing Editor; RICKEY PURDIN, Director of Talent Relations; JENNIFER GRÜNWALD, Senior Editor, Special Projects; SUSAN CRESPI, Production Manager; STAN LEE, Chairman Emeritus. For information regarding advertising in Marvel Comics or on Marvel.com, please contact Vit DeBellis, Custom Solutions & Integrated Advertising Manager, at vdebellis@marvel.com. For Marvel subscription inquiries, please call 888-511-5480. **Manufactured between 12/25/2020 and 1/26/2021 by SOLISCO PRINTERS, SCOTT, QC, CANADA.**

10 9 8 7 6 5 4 3 2 1

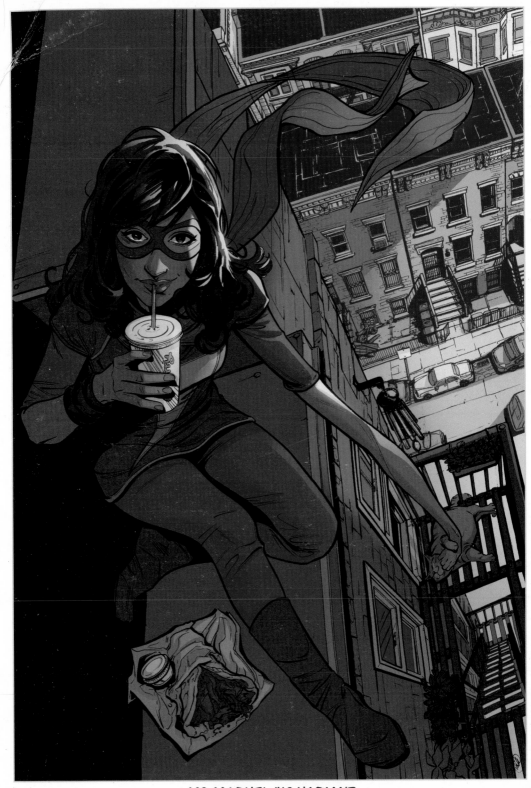

MS. MARVEL #12 VARIANT
BY JOËLLE JONES & RACHELLE ROSENBERG

MS. MARVEL #12 TEASER VARIANT
BY MIKE DEODATO JR. & FRANK MARTIN

MS. MARVEL #10 MARVEL TSUM TSUM TAKEOVER VARIANT
BY TRADD MOORE & MATTHEW WILSON

MS. MARVEL #8 CIVIL WAR REENACTMENT VARIANT
BY SIYA OUM

MS. MARVEL #7 AGE OF APOCALYPSE VARIANT
BY PASQUAL FERRY & CHRIS SOTOMAYOR

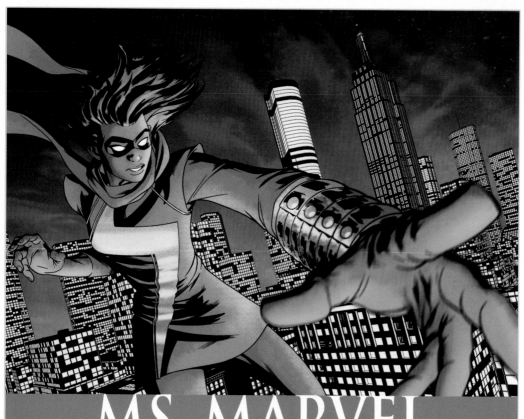

MS. MARVEL
A MARVEL COMICS EVENT

CIVIL
WAR

MS. MARVEL #6 CIVIL WAR VARIANT
BY MIKE McKONE

MS. MARVEL #5 WOMEN OF POWER VARIANT
BY EMA LUPACCHINO & GURU-eFX

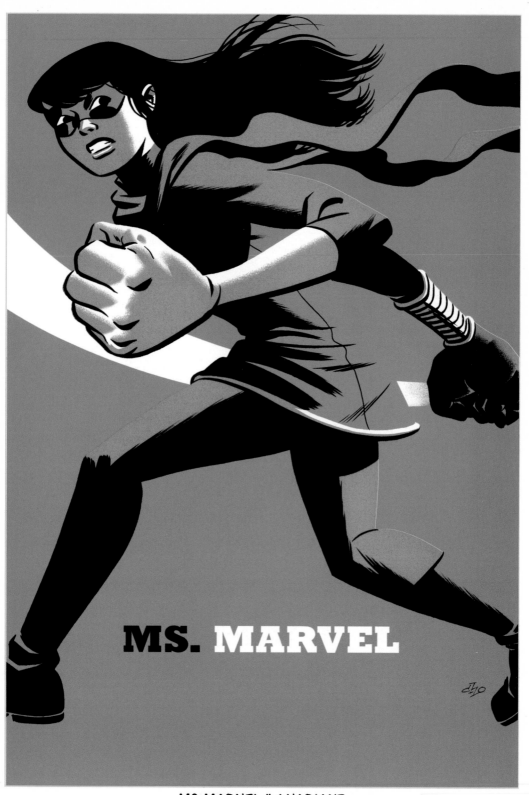

MS. MARVEL #4 VARIANT
BY MICHAEL CHO

MS. MARVEL #3 VARIANT
BY BABS TARR

MS. MARVEL #2 MAVEL '92 VARIANT
BY J. SCOTT CAMPBELL & NEI RUFFINO

MS. MARVEL #2 VARIANT
BY TAKESHI MIYAZAWA & IAN HERRING

MS. MARVEL #2 VARIANT
BY FRED HEMBECK & RACHELLE ROSENBERG

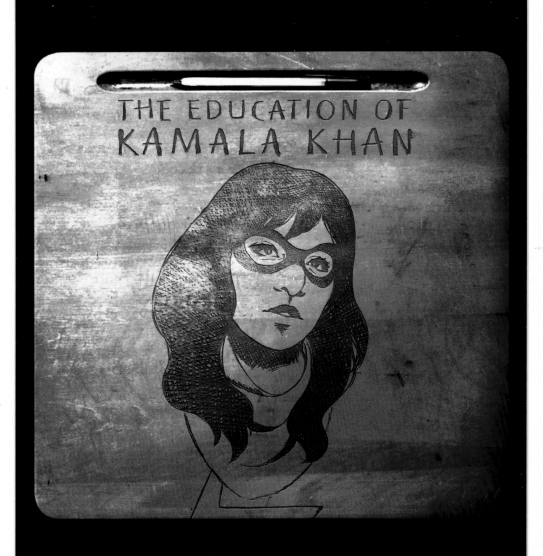

THE EDUCATION OF
KAMALA KHAN

MS. MARVEL #1 HIP-HOP VARIANT
BY JENNY FRISON

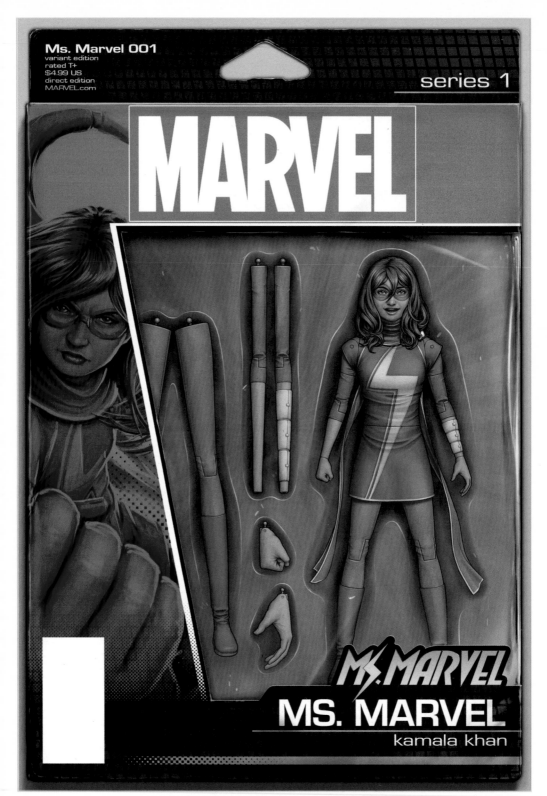

MS. MARVEL #1 ACTION FIGURE VARIANT
BY JOHN TYLER CHRISTOPHER

MS. MARVEL #1 VARIANT
BY SARA PICHELLI & JUSTIN PONSOR

I...I didn't realize that.

Well... you wouldn't, being a ferengi.*

*Foreigner.

How can you tell I'm a ferengi?!

You speak Urdu like someone who *hears* it a lot but doesn't speak it very often.

I guess that's fair.

Look--I know you were trying to help. What you did was very brave. But next time--check in with the *local super heroes* before you destroy a truck.

HE SOUNDS... LIKE *ME*.

Thanks, Red Dagger. This has been weirdly clarifying. I'm really sorry about the mess.

Goodbye, Ms. Marvel. Maybe we'll meet again one day.

I THINK IT'S TIME TO GO BACK TO *JERSEY*.

I DIDN'T FIND THE MISSING PIECES OF MY LIFE IN KARACHI, BECAUSE...

...THE MISSING PIECES AREN'T PART OF A *PLACE*. THEY'RE PART OF *ME*. THEY'RE THINGS ONLY *I* CAN FIGURE OUT.

Who?

...NOT *QUITE* THE REACTION I WAS HOPING FOR.

AND *THEN,* OUT OF NOWHERE...

Throwing knives...get *down!* It's *him!*

SPAK!

WAAAH!

SPAK!

SPAK!

LAAL KHANJEER!*

*The Red Dagger!

Where did you come from? What are *you* doing here?

I could ask *you* the same question!

Karachi is my *home.* I patrol these neighborhoods.

And whoever you are, you're making a *mess* of things. This situation is *complicated.* These bandits might be *dangerous,* but plenty of people who aren't connected to the city's water lines see them as *heroes.*

You have to deal with them *without* destroying any water tankers.

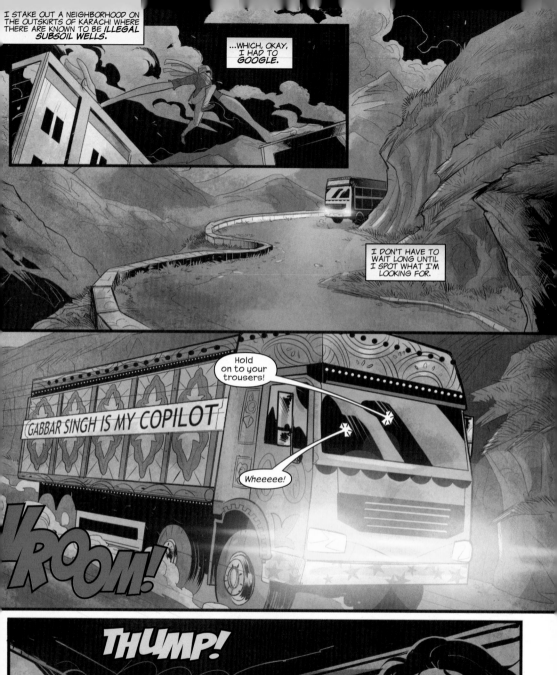

I STAKE OUT A NEIGHBORHOOD ON THE OUTSKIRTS OF KARACHI WHERE THERE ARE KNOWN TO BE *ILLEGAL SUBSOIL WELLS.*

...WHICH, OKAY, I HAD TO *GOOGLE.*

I DON'T HAVE TO WAIT LONG UNTIL I SPOT WHAT I'M LOOKING FOR.

GABBAR SINGH IS MY COPILOT

Hold on to your trousers!

Wheeeee!

VROOM!

THUMP!

Huh?

I STAY IN AND PRAY FAJR* AND DRINK CHAI AND LISTEN TO NAANI'S STORIES.

*Dawn prayer.

I GO OUT AND RIDE HORSES AT CLIFTON BEACH AND DO ALL THE TOURISTY STUFF I WAS TOO YOUNG TO DO LAST TIME I WAS HERE.

I TRY TO SORT OUT MY HEAD.

BUT NO MATTER HOW MANY LISTS I MAKE AND HOW MUCH I CRY ABOUT BRUNO AND CAPTAIN MARVEL AND EVERYTHING THAT'S HAPPENED, I FEEL LIKE I'M *DRIFTING*.

LIKE I EXIST IN SOME KIND OF WEIRD NON-SPACE. IN MY *DREAMS*, I ACCIDENTALLY SHOW UP FOR A MATH EXAM IN MY *COSTUME*, OR I WALK DOWN MUHAMMAD ALI JINNAH ROAD, TURN A CORNER, AND FIND MYSELF BACK IN *JERSEY*.

Huh?

I don't see why I should have to move all my things just because some American girl with a *NICOP card** has--

*A National Identity Card for Pakistanis living abroad and/or dual citizens.

Hellooo. You called?

Oh! Hi! Uh--

That was-- I didn't mean to--

This used to be *my* room, but I'm happy to--to--

It was my *mom's* room way before it was yours.

Who are you, anyway? Are we *related?*

Not technically.

You're Muneeba Khala's daughter, and her sister--your aunt-- went to secondary school with my mother, which would make us...

...*friends- in-law.*

I'm *Kareem.* My family's from *Badin,* but I've been living here while I study for my university entrance exams.

I'm Kamala.

Yes. I know.

I GUESS, THEORETICALLY, THIS WAS KIND OF MY *FIRST HOME.* AMMI WAS PREGNANT WITH ME WHEN SHE AND ABU LEFT FOR JERSEY. AAMIR WAS BORN IN ONE OF THESE ROOMS FIVE YEARS EARLIER.

YEP, *THIS* IS MY HERITAGE, MY *FAMILY HOME,* THE PLACE WHERE I WAS *CONCEIVED...*

Jamilah! The *American* is here!

...AND WHERE I'M KNOWN AS THE KID FROM *SOMEWHERE ELSE.*

Here we are, *jaanu!* This will be your room for the month.

It was *your mother's* room when she was a girl. She used to study for her exams right there on that bed.

Oh wow. I didn't know that.

I'll let you rest and get settled in! Come down for chai when you're ready!

Bahot shukriya, Naani!

First thing's first:

Stick out less.

So that's it? I'm being kicked out of my own room?

Down the hall! The room on the left is empty!

THERE IT IS: NAANI'S BUILDING. I HAVEN'T BEEN HERE SINCE I WAS NINE OR TEN YEARS OLD.

THE WAY AMMI TELLS IT, NAANI AND MY GRANDFATHER MOVED INTO THE TOP FLOOR AS NEWLYWEDS.

THEN, AS THEY HAD KIDS AND THEIR KIDS GOT MARRIED, THEY BOUGHT THE APARTMENT UNDER THAT ONE, AND THE ONE UNDER THAT, UNTIL THE *WHOLE BUILDING* WAS CRAMMED WITH RELATIVES. IT'S BASICALLY *FORTRESS NAANI* NOW.

KAMALA!

...THEY'VE **GOT** TO BE HERE.

Meri jaan! How *big* you've grown!

Oof! Hi, Naani!*

Acha! Such heavy clothes in this heat?

Let me take that!

*Maternal grandmother.

HERE'S THE NICE THING ABOUT *GRANDMAS:*

NO MATTER HOW FAR AWAY THEY LIVE AND HOW LONG IT'S BEEN SINCE YOU SAW THEM LAST, THEY ALWAYS MAKE YOU FEEL LIKE YOU *NEVER LEFT.*

BIRNIN ZANA, WAKANDA

BUT IT *FEELS* LIKE INDEPENDENCE.

ENOUGH ROOM TO BE ALONE, GET AWAY FROM JERSEY FOR A LITTLE WHILE. TRY TO FIGURE OUT HOW SO MANY THINGS GOT SO MESSED UP.

GET AWAY FROM... FROM...

FROM SOME OF THIS *PAIN*.

FROM THE KNOWLEDGE THAT MY BEST FRIEND IS LEAVING TO GET AWAY FROM *ME*.

FROM *EVERYTHING*.

WE'RE ALL *BOUND UP* IN THE PEOPLE WE LOVE--THE PEOPLE WHO MAKE US WHO WE ARE.

SO WHO AM I WITHOUT THEM?

WHO AM I NOW?

STOP IT!

This isn't about *you!*

I have to relearn how to *walk,* Kamala. And I--I can't use my dominant hand, and--

--and what's *worse,* all the schools I was looking at-- all the *scholarships* I was up for--they're *gone.* Nobody wants a guy who accidentally blew up a building.

I'm so sorry, Bruno, I'm so sorry--

No. I don't want your apology. I don't want *anything* from you.

Ever since *Ms. Marvel* came into our lives, it's been like this. Your needs, your problems, your schedule, your rules. It's like I don't matter at all unless I'm *sidekicking* for you.

And when I tried to tell you how crazy the Cadets were getting...you didn't even *listen.*

The only thing that mattered to you was taking orders from Captain Marvel. Nothing else mattered. Your *friends* didn't matter.

I've taken a lot of things for granted. I've taken a lot of *people* for granted. But I can *change*--

This is the life you chose. I'm not asking you to change.

I'm trying to tell you I'm *leaving.*

WHEN VICK CALLS, I ACTUALLY AM ABOUT THREE-QUARTERS ASLEEP.

BUT WHEN HE TELLS ME BRUNO IS BREATHING ON HIS OWN AND SITTING UP, I'M SUDDENLY *WIDE AWAKE*.

Hnngh--

Bruno! You're alive!

Dang it!

Thank God-- I was so *worried*--

Kamala--

Before you say anything--I've *fixed* it. I broke up the *Cadets*, I said some things to *Carol* I can't ever take back--no more predictive justice in Jersey City, not on my watch--

DOOMF!

Rebecca St. Jude, I hereby arrest you on charges of impersonating law enforcement and *kidnapping*.

This isn't over, Ms. Marvel. I'm the *real* hero here, and someday soon, *Carol* is gonna see it.

It's *never* over. But it's over for right now.

Bye, Becky.

Canadian ninjas? *Really?* That seemed like a good idea to you?

I--I can't decide. Maybe?

You're exhausted and your best friend is in danger. You did what you thought you *had* to do. I get that. But you risked *more* lives to do it.

Let's hash it out over a gyro and fries.

Man, that really bums me out.

I think I've reached a point where there is stuff in my life that can't be fixed with a gyro and fries.

I still want the gyro and fries though. Can we take the *Lotus* and drive with the top down?

Sold the Lotus. A lot of things are gonna *change*, kiddo.

Yeah, *bad* change.

Change is what you make of it. Trust yourself. Things'll work out. Maybe not the way you WANT them to, but they will.

I'm trying to protect people, too! Predictive justice is about using the resources we've discovered to save lives. If you can't see that then...

So be it.

Forget her. Forget both of them.

You need a *new* junior partner, and I'm ready to step in...

I've been thinking about a codename... *Lockdown.*

No. You overstepped your bounds, failed to win the trust of the people and *attacked* your commanding officer with lethal force.

Ms. Marvel should have kept you in line, but since she *didn't...* I will.

I have no choice but to have you court-martialed.

SHE DOESN'T SAY GOODBYE.

SHE DOESN'T SAY *ANYTHING.*

ALL THAT'S LEFT IS ME AND THE MESS I'VE MADE.

Bye, Becky.

The next time you show your face in Jersey City will be the *last* time you show your face in Jersey City.

But I thought you'd probably disagree, so--

--I called somebody *else* at the same time I called you.

CHOOM!

RIGHT ABOUT HERE IS WHERE IT OCCURS TO ME...

You brought *him* here?

Carol, listen--

...SHE IS *NEVER* GOING TO FORGIVE ME FOR THIS. NEVER.

AND IT HURTS.

I *trusted* you. You have my *name*, you wear my colors--

--but seeing how far you've gone to make your point, I can see my trust was *misplaced*.

WORSE THAN GETTING PUNCHED IN THE GUT. WORSE THAN HAVING MY HEART BROKEN. WORSE THAN PRETTY MUCH ANYTHING.

I didn't *want* this...

...but I have to protect the people of my city. Even...even if it means protecting them from *you*.

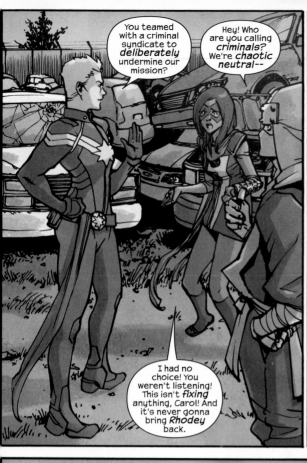

You teamed with a criminal syndicate to *deliberately* undermine our mission?

Hey! Who are you calling *criminals?* We're *chaotic neutral--*

I had no choice! You weren't listening! This isn't *fixing* anything, Carol! And it's never gonna bring *Rhodey* back.

THIS...THIS IS WHERE IT ALL STARTS TO GO TOTALLY OFF THE RAILS.

What did you just say?

Okay, that last part came out totally wrong--

I understood you just fine.

From here on out, I'm taking charge of the Cadets and all further implementation of predictive justice in Jersey City *myself.*

You're lucky I don't hand you over to the *FBI* for aiding and abetting a *criminal syndicate.* You haven't just betrayed your mission-- you've betrayed your own *ethics.*

I--I'm sorry you feel that way.

But see-- here's what I've learned over the past couple of weeks. The world is *messy.* Good guys do bad things. Bad guys do good things. If you lock somebody up before they've even committed a crime, you make them into a bad guy, even if they weren't before.

"Get *off!* Stop it!"

"Down with the capitalist police state!"

BONK!

CLANG

BONK!

CLANG

BOOM!

"I assume you wanted me to make an entrance, since you activated your *locator pendant?*"

"Yeah, I did. I wanted you to see this."

"What's happening here? Is everyone okay?"

"I asked Hijinx and his crew to stage a crime. To prove that predictive justice can be *rigged.*"

"Which you'd already know if you saw that one movie with that *short actor*--"

CHOOM!

Ninja syndicate! **ATTACK!**

TORONTO HARD STYLE: MAPLE LEAF FORMATION!

Huh?!

WELL, CAN'T ARGUE WITH THAT.

You think you're so *noble*, but you're NOT--you're endangering innocent lives so you can *coddle criminals.*

No one is a criminal until they've committed a crime. You want to make *more* criminals? Lock people up before they've done anything wrong.

Hnngh!

WHOOOAAA!

WHOMP!

Ugh!

Anyone who helps criminals is *also* a criminal.

You're gonna get what you *deserve...*

Nothing inside. It's *fake*.

I don't get it. What's going on here? Ulysses said Hijinx planted bombs all over this lot--

And he was *wrong*. This was a *setup*-- Hijinx planted *fake* explosives to lure you here.

But *why?*

So that you--and more importantly, Captain Marvel-- could see how *broken* predictive justice really is.

It can be used to *entrap* people, set people up, cause mistaken identities--

--because no matter how accurate Ulysses' visions are, they're still interpreted by *humans,* and humans are *biased.*

Cute. Very cute. Did you read that in an *anthropology textbook?*

You wanna know what *I* see going on here?

I see Jersey City's homegrown hero turning *traitor.*

BOOM!

You--you *liar!* We agreed there'd be *no violence!* That was the whole *point!*

Sorry. I had to blow up *one* thing. Otherwise it wouldn't have been *convincing.* You know how psychics are with their *time paradoxes*--

You see? You *think* you're in control of this. But you're not.

This is where I say "say hello to my little friends"!

And you *duck.*

OH BOY. THIS IS GONNA HURT.

You think you're so funny--

Hey! *Bigfoot!* This is your cue!

S T O M P!

Let Hijinx go. You're gonna have to deal with *me* instead.

Well, well, well. A wild *Ms. Marvel* appears.

Freeing criminals instead of locking them up is becoming a *habit,* I see.

Not *this* time.

Hijinx, show her the *detonator.*

SLEEP IS GOING TO HAVE TO WAIT.

EXHAUSTED AS I AM, I CAN'T LET THIS STAND.

BASIC BECKY *CAN'T* BE ALLOWED TO IMPRISON MORE PEOPLE FOR CRIMES THEY HAVEN'T EVEN COMMITTED YET. SHE CAN'T BE ALLOWED TO DESTROY MORE FAMILIES, MORE LIVES...

THIS IS NOW AN "AT ALL COSTS" KIND OF SITUATION.

I *WILL* STOP HER. I *WILL* PUT AN END TO *PREDICTIVE IN-JUSTICE.*

EVEN IF IT MEANS BETRAYING THE ONE PERSON I ADMIRE MOST ON THIS EARTH.

"...so she'll always be safe."

Hey, Kamala.

Hey, Vick.

You should go home and *sleep* or something. I'll stay here until Bruno's out of surgery.

Nah, I'll stay too. I'm not tired.

Liar. Go sleep. It's cool, I'll take care of stuff.

I can't. They said they won't know if--if he's gonna make it until they take the breathing tube out. I *have* to stay 'til then.

I'll call you as *soon* as that happens, I swear. You need to lie down--you look *awful.*

If you say so.

I'll be back *soon*, okay?

I just-- I just can't do any of this *without* you--

WHOOP WHOOP WHOOP!

Huh?!

BUT THE FUTURE KEEPS UNDOING ITSELF, EVEN WITH ME STANDING RIGHT THERE, READY TO FIX THINGS.

IT JUST KEEPS UNRAVELING.

Clear the room! He's *crashing!*

AND UNRAVELING.

I've got a pulse--it's *weak--*

Someone tell the O.R. we have an *emergency!*

UNTIL ALL THAT'S LEFT IS *ME*, HOLDING A PILE OF STRING.

LATER. I'VE JUST DECIDED I'M NOT GONNA SLEEP.

NOT TONIGHT, ANYWAY. MAYBE NOT EVER.

MY WHOLE LIFE IS LIKE A *SWEATER UNRAVELING.* IF I CAN JUST PAY ATTENTION LONG ENOUGH TO CATCH THE THREAD, MAYBE I CAN *STOP* IT, AND PUT EVERYTHING BACK THE WAY IT *WAS.*

Kamala! You're finally here--

Don't get up, Nonna. I'm just gonna say hi.

He hasn't regained consciousness. The doctors are *worried.*

I don't understand *why* this is happening, Kamala. Bruno is such a good boy-- now everything is mixed up--

Bruno? It's me. You've gotta wake up. Everybody's freaking out.

I know things have been weird recently, but-- I'm *fixing* it. I've taken a lot of stuff--a lot of *people,* for granted. And it's not okay.

It was a stupid plan anyway...

WHAM!

Ulp!

You've got some nerve coming here after what happened yesterday.

I spent the whole afternoon in a cell, being yelled at by your little police state youth brigade. Whatever you came here for, the answer is no.

What if I said I want you to plan a crime?

Go on.

IT DOESN'T TAKE ME LONG TO COME UP WITH THE BEGINNING OF A *PLAN.*

ONE THAT INVOLVES WADING INTO THE TERRITORY OF THE *CANADIAN NINJA SYNDICATE* AFTER JUST HAVING ROYALLY PISSED OFF THEIR LEADER.

CRUNCH!

THIS MAY OR MAY NOT BE A TERRIBLE IDEA.

BUT IF I CAN PROVE TO CAPTAIN MARVEL THAT PREDICTIVE JUSTICE IS *FLAWED*-- THAT IT CAN BE *RIGGED,* THAT IT CAN *CREATE* THE PROBLEMS IT'S SUPPOSED TO SOLVE--

I'm looking for *Hijinx!*

Come out, come out wherever you are! We need to *talk!*

THEN MAYBE SHE'LL REALIZE HOW *WRONG* ALL THIS IS. AND THINGS CAN GO BACK TO *NORMAL...*

What-- where is she going?

The pressure's too much for her. She's starting to *snap.*

Changing the future is a big responsibility.

Some people are too sentimental to handle it.

Ms. Marvel gets caught up in the excuses and sob stories of people who are too *lazy* and *entitled* to pull their lives together.

It makes her *weak.*

We've seen it.

And now, *Captain Marvel* sees it too.

It's only a matter of time before they're at each other's *throats.*

And that's when I'll make my move.

What do you mean we can't?!

Excluding today, you and the Cadets have been an amazing success. Proof that predictive justice *can* work.

And...and I *need* it to work...

Ever since *Rhodey* died...

Tony-- Iron Man-- we haven't been getting along very well.

I know. It feels like my *super hero parents* are getting *divorced*.

And I'm *sorry* about that, Junior-- I really am.

I know things are *chaotic* right now. I know you're hurting. But we *have* to get through this together-- otherwise it will all have been for nothing.

I'll be back as soon as I take care of a few things across the river. Can I count on you until then?

HOW CAN I SAY NO?

BUT...HOW CAN I SAY *YES?*

You heard the boss...back to work.

SHE'S RIGHT. IT *IS* TIME TO GET BACK TO WORK.

AND I *DON'T* WORK FOR BASIC BECKY.

What do we do?!

Call her.

But-- Call her.

Call her.

WHOOSH!

You know what I've always thought is *funny* about your powers?

You exert so much *force* that you have to spend as much time trying *not* to hurt people as you do *actually fighting.*

WHOOSH!

Nnngh!

Like right now, you could totally just *stomp* on me, but I know you're not--

--huh?

WHAM!

WHOA. OKAY.

Plasma armor. Custom made. Isn't it awesome?

Hnngh--

Guys, I really don't think--

Oof!

WHAFF!

How come Ulysses didn't know?

How come he knew that *Josh* was planning to *attack* Coles Academic, but not that *Bruno* was going to end up in a *coma* trying to free him?

That's not how it works. He's not *omniscient.*

Trying to override an electromagnetic lock with *more* electricity is just *dumb*, especially for a genius.

By mounting that silly rescue mission, your friend changed the timeline. That's *his* fault, not Ulysses'.

His fault? He was trying to get his friend out of extra-legal detention, and it's his fault?

Yeah, we put Josh Richardson in a cell overnight. And saved dozens of lives in the process.

And who *authorized* us to keep him there, even after that Bruno kid got mad about it?

JOSH...BRUNO... I COULD HAVE *STOPPED* THIS.

You're right. This is my fault.

I was put in charge of this experiment.

And now I'm shutting it *down.*

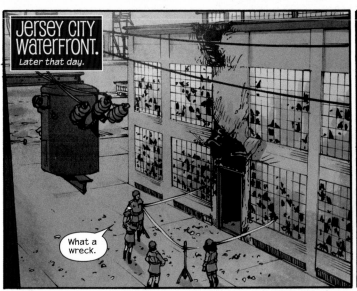

JERSEY CITY WATERFRONT.
Later that day.

What a wreck.

Base of operations destroyed, prisoners *escaped*, police and press crawling all over the place--

It's like people don't *want* a safer world--

WOMP!

If he **lives**, he might walk again, with physical therapy, but there'll be some **lingering paralysis** on his left side.

And he's **lost** the use of that hand.

But he's left-handed! He **makes** things-- that's his **life**--if he can't work in the lab, he'll--

I can't believe this is happening--

Do you-- uhh--need some time **alone**, or something?

I need to **erase** the past twenty-four hours and **start over**.

ALL OF A SUDDEN, IT FEELS LIKE I'VE BEEN PLAYING **PRETEND**.

DRESSING UP AS A MAKE-BELIEVE SUPER HERO AND FIGHTING MAKE-BELIEVE CRIME.

AND NOW...

...NOW IT'S **REAL.** VERY, VERY REAL.

BECAUSE WHY WOULD HE PASS UP A CHANCE TO SHOW OFF HOW *SMART* HE IS.

THAT'S A RHETORICAL QUESTION, BY THE WAY.

WHEN I GET DONE *YELLING* AT HIM, HE IS GONNA--

CLICK!

Hunh?!

KABOOM!

Bruno? BRUNO!

Say something! Please--

Ka- Kamala--

FOR A SECOND, I THINK, IT'S OKAY. HE'S OKAY.

SO IT'S COME TO THIS.

When I get ahold of that boy, I am gonna say some *things*...

MY *BEST FRIEND* HAS GONE BEHIND MY BACK TO DO SOMETHING I EXPLICITLY ASKED HIM *NOT* TO DO.

AND NOW, I'M GONNA *MESS UP* IN FRONT OF CAROL, WHO WILL NEVER TRUST ME WITH SUCH A *BIG RESPONSIBILITY* EVER AGAIN...

HE COULDN'T JUST *WAIT?* HE COULDN'T JUST LET IT GO AND LET *ME* HANDLE IT?

WHEN DID HE AND STUPID *JOSH* GET SO *CLOSE*, ANYWAY?

THE CADETS PUT AN *ELECTROMAGNETIC LOCK* ON THE DOOR OF THE WAREHOUSE TO MAKE IT HARDER TO BREAK INTO.

AND KNOWING BRUNO, HE PROBABLY BUILT SOME SORT OF FANCY-PANTS DEVICE OUT OF PAPER CLIPS AND CHEWING GUM TO GET THROUGH IT.

I'm worried about **Kamala**.

Hmm?

She seems *exhausted.* And those *friends* of hers used to be in and out of the house all the time, but now she's always *alone.*

Maybe she's just *studying a lot* or something.

Aamir.

Okay, okay.

Hey. Booger. Wake up.

Hnngh?

You'll get a crick in your neck if you sleep out here. Go pray *Isha** and head to bed. Tyesha and I already did the dishes.

The night prayer, performed after twilight.

Nooo... I was getting to the good part of my *dream...*

Whatever, *pagal.*

Oh yeah-- *Bruno* called earlier. He said something about going to get *Josh?* I didn't really understand. I told him you'd call--

--back.

We have a *situation* here. There is a big crowd of people outside who want *answers,* and we've gotta come up with some, *fast.*

Captain Marvel put *me* in charge of this mess, so from now on, I get the final say in what we do with the information *Ulysses* gives us.

Which means we clear this little operation with the *police,* so there's no more *confusion.* This is supposed to be about...*upholding* the law, not *breaking* it.

This is *not* gonna end well.

What about *Josh?*

Josh *stays.* He's too big of a *risk.* I'll make sure he has what he needs between now and the future-that-no-longer-happens.

I can't believe this! You're gonna side with *Basic Becky* and the *Junior Fascists* against your own *friends?!*

Hey now!

Come on, Bruno. Let's get out of here.

We're *not* Ms. Marvel's friends.

We're *background characters.*

Everybody just *hold on* a minute--I'll get all this stuff sorted out, I *promise*--

If I could just get a statement--

Bye bye!

So you'd rather endanger the lives of *dozens* of people than keep *one* damaged guy in a cell overnight?

We're not even sure Josh really would have gone through with it. He needs *counseling*.

If he's messed up, keeping him in a concrete room by himself isn't gonna make him *less* messed up.

Guys--

You can't *lock* somebody up for a crime they haven't committed yet. That's *not* how justice works. Better to let a hundred guilty men go free than condemn one innocent--

You want to let people *die* to prove a *point?* That's what you call justice?

GUYS!

My *grandson* is in there! No one will tell me what he's done *wrong!*

Stay calm, everybody stay calm. Let us do our *jobs*...

--at an abandoned warehouse on the Jersey City waterfront, where rumor has it that *Ms. Marvel* and unknown associates are holding as many as a dozen people *without* formal charges--

VRRRRRRRMM!

Uh-oh.

Ms. Marvel! You've got to tell us what's going on!

Ms. Marvel, can you confirm for our viewers that you or your delegates are holding Jersey City citizens inside this warehouse *extralegally?*

So...then...
who *do*
you like?

SNAPPY THE ~~ATOR~~

Oh.

I *never* wanted to burn down the school. I just wanted to *scare* people. Then, maybe they would *respect* me.

I know that sounds crazy.

Yeah, it kind of *does*.

So were you really going to go through with it?

I don't know. It's the *future*. Something must *happen* between now and tomorrow to make up my mind.

Really, I just wanted to talk to *you*. I still don't understand why I'm not good enough anymore...

Josh...when we broke up... it had *nothing* to do with you. Seriously.

The whole *world almost ending* thing made me think about a bunch of stuff. I realized I had to be *honest* about some things.

I don't... I don't like *boys*, Josh.

I never really have. But they've always liked *me*, so I just sort of...went with the program.

I know I was *super mean* to you a lot when we were going out, but it *wasn't* because I thought you were stupid.

If anything, I was angry at *myself*.

Oh.

I...thanks for telling me. It must have been hard for you. But... a lot of stuff makes *sense* now.

Zoe?! Don't "Zoe" me! Were you seriously planning to fry the school's power grid because I broke up with you?! What kind of demented sicko logic is that?!

Open this door.

You don't have the authority to--

My mom is a lawyer and my dad is on the City Council. Take it up with them.

Open.

This.

Door.

You've got five minutes.

We'll just, uhh...give you guys some space for a second.

I am so flipping angry at you right now.

I--

You can't be with me, so no one can be with me? Is that it? Is that the "yeah, bro" deep thought that was going through your head when you decided burning down the school was a good idea?

No! It's not like that!

I didn't want to hurt anybody, I just--

I just wanted them to see how much I'm hurting.

I demand extradition to Canada! I don't recognize your authority or that of your imperialist government!

Save it, *Hijinx.*

B13

Hey--

What? What's wrong?

We may have a *problem.* The press suspects we've been *lying* about having the authority to detain people here.

I *knew* that stupid newscast last night was going to cause us trouble...

What do we do?

If they come here looking for answers, we can give them *Hijinx...*he's not an immediate threat anymore.

But *Mr. Varsity Linebacker* over there *stays.*

Until 10 A.M. tomorrow, he's a *potential terrorist.*

We demand to see *Joshua Richardson,* who is being held here *illegally!*

Josh! You idiot! What have you *done?!*

Sorry, Becky... we *tried* to keep them out...

--if we only hold people we *don't* like accountable, we're not on the side of *justice.*

You have to be strong now. Do what's *right*, even if it hurts.

I'm *trying.* But Becky pulled a *taser* on this guy earlier--

I'm worried the Cadets are getting out of line.

Then you *keep* them in line. That's your job.

Can I count on you to see this through?

Of course. Of course you can.

YOU CAN COUNT ON ME...BUT PART OF ME IS WONDERING...

Good. You're *dismissed.*

...IF I CAN STILL COUNT ON YOU.

BUT I KNOW SOMEONE WHO CAN.

FSST!

Captain Marvel, we need to *talk*.

Junior? What're you doing up here?

The Cadets and I went to bust some kid who was planning to *melt* his own high school and I was totally cool with it but then I found out this kid is my *friend* and he hasn't actually *done* anything *wrong* yet and now I don't know what to do--

Whoa, whoa. Slow down.

This was *never* going to be easy or simple, kiddo.

And I'm sorry your friend is in trouble, but--

This is outrageous!

Ms. Marvel, you have to *help* him--you were *there* at the school during the *Incursion*, you saw the way Josh helped and protected people-- he's a good boy--

I'm sorry, Mr. and Mrs. Richardson, I promise I'll do what I can--

IT WASN'T SUPPOSED TO LOOK LIKE THIS.

Hey! You can't kidnap me from my own house! I demand a *lawyer!*

Not happening.

IT WAS SUPPOSED TO BE *GLORIOUS.*

Future crimes are under *new* jurisdiction.

ACK!

BUT IT ISN'T.

AND I DON'T KNOW HOW TO FIX IT.

"...and one day, when it is *most* needed...

"...it will *appear.*"

Big M? What... what are you doing here?

ON THE GROUND! NOW!

Huh?!

Wait! Stop! Don't hurt him!

Hnngh!

CRASH!

OWW!

Joshua Richardson, we're *detaining* you to prevent the crime you are about to commit.

Read me the address!

437 Nelson Place...it's in Hamilton Park...

'Scuse me! Sorry!

No problem, Big M!

AS I TURN THE CORNER ONTO NELSON PLACE, I CAN'T SHAKE THE FEELING I'VE *BEEN HERE* BEFORE.

FOR A SCHOOL THING? A PARTY? A GROUP PROJECT? I CAN'T PLACE IT, BUT...

...I HAVE THE *WEIRDEST* FEELING...

CRASH!

AAAH!

What's going on here?!

Your *son!* Where's his room?

S-second door on the left--

Maybe you should try thinking about *law-abiding stuff* instead.

But I--

Ms. Marvel! You've got to come with us!

Kinda *busy* right this second, guys--

This is *BIG!* We have an hour--less-- *minutes*--

Teenage male, blond, athletic--

If we don't get to the address Ulysses sent me within the next few minutes, Coles Academic High School is going to be *vaporized.*

Ulysses doesn't know *how*, only that it's gonna *happen*--

THIS?

THIS IS ONE OF THOSE WORST CASE SCENARIOS I PROBABLY *SHOULD* PLAN FOR, BUT NEVER DO.

IF I CAN STOP *THIS* FROM HAPPENING...

So am I, like, *under arrest* or what?

Hello?

...THEN *EVERYTHING* ELSE IS WORTH IT.

MAYBE ULYSSES IS A *ROBOT*.

A COMPUTER PROGRAM. NO PERSON, *INHUMAN* OR NOT, IS *RIGHT* ABOUT SO MUCH, SO OFTEN.

FOR DAYS, THIS IS WHAT I DO.

WAIT FOR A TIP FROM THE *CADETS*. STAKE OUT THE SCENE OF A CRIME THAT *NEVER HAPPENS*.

THEY NEVER EXPECT ME.

GAAH!

WHOMP!

WHY WOULD THEY? THEY THINK THEY'RE *ALONE* WITH THEIR THOUGHTS.

Sorry, random dude.

You don't get to rob grocery stores on *my* watch.

How did you know?!

I was just *thinking* about it!

You're *smarter* than this, Kamala.

Don't go, Tyesha! I had a really weird day! I need a *hug!*

Aww. Baby girl.

I love you. But *don't* fall for this stuff. Please.

But Tyesha--this *new* system--what if it saves lives?

Whose lives?

Did you ever think that maybe the people *committing* the crimes need saving *too?*

...and now, the *weather* report.

Earlier today, the crime lord known only as Hijinx, leader of a Toronto-based *smuggling ring*, was apprehended by *Ms. Marvel* and a cadre of *assistants*.

HIJINX

CANADIAN NINJA LEADER APPRE

Though the experimental military equipment stolen by Hijinx was destroyed during a high-speed chase, no one was seriously injured.

Ms. Marvel and her--

This *isn't* gonna end well.

Weird. You're the *second* person who's said that today.

Well it's *true*. If they prosecute this Hijinx guy for something he *might* have done with that tank, we'll have to *redefine* what we call crime.

Tyesha, if he was *planning* to do something terrible with it, isn't it better to get him off the streets *before* he hurts somebody?

You want me to tell you what *Greenville* was like when I was growing up? During the whole *tough-on-crime* thing?

Boys could get picked up for standing on a street corner for too long. *Probable cause*, right?

Know what it got us? A whole generation of kids who went to jail instead of *college*.

JUST A FEW HOURS LATER, BECKY GETS HER FIRST TIP FROM *ULYSSES*, WHO I GUESS IS THEORETICALLY RIGHT ACROSS THE RIVER IN NEW ATTILAN.

NEW JERSEY WASTE MANAGEMENT

APPARENTLY, *HIJINX*, LEADER OF THE CANADIAN NINJA SYNDICATE, IS ABOUT TO DRIVE A TANK STOLEN FROM A TOP-SECRET MILITARY FACILITY RIGHT THROUGH DOWNTOWN JERSEY CITY.

IF WE DON'T STOP HIM, IN 17 MINUTES, THE TANK'S *AUTO-DESTRUCT* SEQUENCE WILL KICK IN, AND IT WILL *EXPLODE.*

This is it. He's gonna turn down this street within the next 90 seconds.

Wow. You guys have had some *athletic training.*

Crossfit, baby!

Are you...you know...one of those funky *disaster over-preparedness* people?

Preppers? Nah. But we do like to be *prepared,* if you know what I mean.

Clear comms, please. We're gonna *nail* this guy any second now.

I seriously doubt the leader of the Canadian Ninja Syndicate would just *randomly--*

Fair enough! I'll let the rest of the squad introduce themselves...

Heather here! I study *information security systems*.

Hey, I'm Jonah. I study *criminal justice* at Rutgers.

I'm Marco. I'm *lactose intolerant*.

Wow! That was like *group therapy*...

We're eager to get to *work*.

I know we're going to have to figure stuff out along the way.

I think of Jersey City like a *test case* for predictive justice... how will it *work* in a city with a historically high crime rate?

Hey! What are you *implying*?!

Oh my gosh, nothing! I phrased that *poorly*.

I just meant that it'll be interesting to see what kind of *difference* we can make in a city like this.

AND JUST LIKE THAT...

There are a lot of *bad people* out there in the world, doing *terrible* things.

I'm just happy we can finally do something about it.

...I HAVE SIDEKICKS.

I will do what you ask. With honor, commitment, courage, and all the other stuff.

I know you will. But--

--Becky and her friends are *new* at this. Until we understand exactly how Ulysses' powers work, they need to stay within the *law*.

LIBERTY STATE PARK. *Later that day.*

"Make sure they *know* that."

So...you're Ms. Marvel. *The* Ms. Marvel. I'm *Becky*.

This is *really* exciting.

Yes. It is *I*. Ms. Marvel.

But let's skip the gushing because it gets weird pretty fast...

This is going to change *everything*.

I *knew* I could count on you to understand how *important* this is.

So...can I ask you to do something for me? Something *big*?

Totally. Anything. I'm so ready.

Good.

This is *Becky St. Jude*.

She's put together a team of *vetted volunteers* who are eager to put Ulysses' knowledge to good use.

They each have *unique skill sets* that will be useful to this mission.

So like... they're the Carol... *Cadets*?

I guess you could say that, sure.

They'll need *supervision*. Someone to liaise between the volunteers, the Inhumans, and *me*.

I can think of exactly *one person* who fits that bill.

I have been *waiting* for this moment.

Listen-- you know about the new *Inhuman* Medusa's people found?

Yeah. *Ulysses.* Isn't he supposed to be, like, the most ultra powerful future-telling clairvoyant person ever?

Not quite. What Ulysses does isn't magic. It's more like *mathematics*--he can determine, to within a fraction of a percent, the probability that certain events are going to take place.

He's an *opportunity.* An opportunity for us to fight crime *without* violence. To stop tragedies before they happen. Imagine how life could change...how *our* lives could change.

We wouldn't just be saving civilians. We'd be saving police officers, firefighters. *Heroes.*

NO MORE NARROW ESCAPES. NO MORE WORRYING ABOUT WHETHER MY FRIENDS MADE IT OUT *ALIVE.*

NO MORE *BREAKING CURFEW.*

That would be... amazing.

You're right. It *would* be.

But not everyone down there sees this the way we do. People--governments, some of your teammates on the *Avengers* -- have *concerns.*

We'd be detaining people before they commit crimes, instead of after the damage has been done. It's uncomfortable.

That sounds a lot like *profiling.*

Profiling was *bad science.* You can't always predict who is going to commit a crime based on some subjective data about *a whole community.*

This is different. Ulysses can isolate *individuals.* Not communities, not families...*specific* people.

APPARENTLY, **GOING TO SPACE** IS A THING I DO NOW.

ALPHA FLIGHT LOW-ORBIT SPACE STATION. *Present Day.*

I PROBABLY DON'T NEED TO TELL YOU HOW **NERVOUS** I AM.

I'M GOING TO SEE **CAPTAIN MARVEL,** WHO HAS A "TIME-SENSITIVE MATTER REQUIRING THE UTMOST DISCRETION" TO DISCUSS WITH ME.

You know, the **aerolith** is equipped with its own **mini-gravity shields** to keep the g-force from knocking you out when it zooms up and down.

AURORA

PUCK

Best day ever.

She's right through there.

Good luck!

Hey, kiddo. Glad you made it.

I totally got *airsick* in the aerolith on the way up. Please don't tell anybody.

I would *never.*

LATER.

Madison Square Garden was evacuated this afternoon when a teen's project unexpectedly *exploded* at the annual tristate science fair.

No one was seriously injured, but damage to the interior of the event center was *extensive.*

The culprit was a *miniature fusion reactor* created by Jersey City high schooler *Bruno Carrelli,* a local boy genius.

More on this story as events unfold.

NEW ATTILAN.
Capital city of the Inhumans.

Trying to stay *connected,* Ulysses? To your old life, your old world?

Yeah. It's just...I'm trying to remember that it's all still *real.* You, us, the Inhumans, my powers--it's all been *amazing,* but I keep having to remind myself that the world keeps turning even though everything I know has *changed.*

You'll get used to it. This is your home, your *family*--we'll teach you *whatever* you want to know.

I know, Medusa. And I--

Wait. Don't change the channel.

Ulysses? What is it? Another *premonition?*

I'm not sure.

But I think maybe... something very big is about to happen...

*Traditional West African formal attire for men.

You're only one person. Superhuman is still *human.*

It's okay to say no to things. Really.

But I *like* saying yes to all the things.

I've noticed.

Think of it as *prioritizing,* then. Thirty years from now, what will you be sorry you missed?

AND JUST LIKE THAT, IT'S OBVIOUS.

I--I have somewhere to be.

AAMIR. AAMIR IS GETTING *MARRIED.* AND I WAS GOING TO *SKIP* IT.

Hold up for a minute.

Uh-oh.

Does this mean you're in trouble?

I seriously hope not.

Geez, kid, what the heck are you getting into down here? I just saw half of Jersey City light up from *low orbit.*

Is there a problem?

I don't know-- your teammate is so *overworked* that she just caused a minor catastrophe in a major metropolitan area, would you consider that a problem?

COME ON, CAROL.

PLEASE DON'T LET ME DOWN.

WHAT AM I GONNA DO IF SHE *DOESN'T* SHOW UP?

IS THIS LEGIT THE *END* OF MS. MARVEL? HOW CAN I BE A SUPER HERO IF I CAN'T EVEN PROTECT MY OWN CITY FROM A THREAT *I* CREATED?

MAYBE THERE'S SOMETHING I *MISSED*. MAYBE THERE'S A WAY TO MAKE THIS RIGHT I JUST HAVEN'T FIGURED OUT YET...

...THEN AGAIN, MAYBE *NOT*.

I'd just like to state that I'm sort of *uncomfortable with this.*

Even if either of us *did* believe in magic, none of this stuff corresponds to any *actual* known belief system.

I know, I know. But we messed up, and then we *messed up* trying to fix the mess-up, and now I think it's time for our *fall-back option.*

But how do you know he'll even show up?

I *don't!* But if *I* were some kind of all-powerful hipster viking, I'd *know* when somebody was trying to get my attention, even if the way they were doing it was sort of--uhh-- *unorthodox.*

Loki, God of-- whatever it is!

Hear us in our hour of need! We tried to *reverse engineer* your weirdo golem-thingies, and our prideful works have rebounded upon us tenfold!

Next he'll grow a giant beard and start speaking in *tongues.*

Will he?

Listen-- I have an *idea.* What if, instead of trying to take out the bizarro Kamala clones one by one, we make something really *big* to take them *all* out at once?!

I've been messing around with the *Beastron*, and I think I could use hipster viking goop to create, like, a *super-predator* or something, you know, like a *giant T.rex...*

You want to make a *giant dinosaur* to eat all the clones.

Are you *five years old?*

Oh. Uhh-- So what I'm hearing is that you don't think it's a good idea. Okay. All right.

That's-- that's--

Don't tell me you already *did* it!

Uhh...

MENACE!!

6

MEANWHILE.

FOR SOME REASON, MY PHONE HASN'T STOPPED RINGING ALL DAY.

ACTUALLY, *PHONES*, PLURAL. NAKIA AND ZOE AND AMMI ON MY CIVILIAN PHONE, BRUNO ON *BOTH* MY PHONES--

RRRING RRING!

WHY CAN'T PEOPLE JUST *RESPECT* MY *SPACE*?

WHY IS IT THAT WHEN I TRY TO PURSUE *MY* GOALS FOR FIVE MINUTES, EVERYBODY DECIDES THEY NEED MY ATTENTION *IMMEDIATELY*?

SPAK
SPAK
SPAK!

Are you going to *answer* that already?

This is getting *really* annoying!

RRRING RRING!

Not a chance!

Forget the phone-- look behind you!

Yeah, right. You just want me to let down my guard--

BUT THEN, I HEAR IT.

Huh?!

THE SOUND OF DOZENS OF FOOTSTEPS...

Kamala! *Finally!* Sit down and stop grinning like an imbecile!

Pardon my daughter. She likes to make an *entrance.* As I was saying, we were *also* concerned when Aamir brought home a girl we'd never met. A girl from a very--*different* background.

But we were *impressed* by Tyesha. Such a mature, steady young lady. A credit to you and your wife, sir.

The world is changing. My generation...we were *not* ready for certain things. But our *children* are.

And if Tyesha wants to join this family, then sir, I will treat her as my *own* flesh and blood.

Then I say... long live the *Hillman-Khans.*

We're gonna be *sisters!*

Shaadi mubarak

*Congrats on the wedding!

This is my **work phone**, Bruno. We don't use *that name* on my work phone.

Okay, whatever! Listen, we've got a *big problem*. You know your little *doppelganger golems*?

Yeah.

They've **spawned**.

Mmmph!

Spawned? What do you mean, *"spawned"*?

I mean they've **multiplied**! There's a bunch of them now!

How is that even possible?

I have no idea!

A flaw in my design? A mistake during the 3D printing process? Outside **contamination**?

Okay. So can you fix it?.

I dunno...all I know is that they're trashing the science lab, and I have to get them out of here before people show up for class.

You've gotta **help** me!

ON AN ORDINARY MORNING I'D BE TRYING TO FINISH MY HOMEWORK, ICING WHATEVER BRUISES I PICKED UP FROM *SUPER-HEROING* THE NIGHT BEFORE, AND ATTEMPTING TO GET TO SCHOOL ON TIME.

You've interfered with our operations for too long, Ms. Marvel.

BUT TODAY...

...TODAY I FEEL *FREE.*

THONK!

Hnngh!

RRRNING!

Hello?

AAAH!

Kamala! You've got to get down here! There are--

"But what I can't figure out is... busy with *what?*"

AAAAAH man these early shifts are killing me--

GO School !!!

Shaadi mubarakbad!

Easy peasy!

--ooooh, crap.

Easy peasy!

Easy peasy!

Shaadi mubarakbad!

So I think I'm gonna take a second stab at going *vegan.*

Eww, why?

I saw this documentary about the way *cow farts* are destroying the atmosphere? And I thought, like, I need to be responsible about my consumption of meat and dairy.

Zoe Zimmer wants to be a responsible consumer.

My baby is growing up.

Staaaahhhp!

Hey, Kamala. How're things?

Easy peasy!

Oh. Okay. *Good.*

What's gotten into *her?*

I don't know, Zo. Sometimes I feel like she's just on *autopilot.* She's always so *busy...*

You're a lifesaver, Bruno! I'll be back to pick these guys up tomorrow morning!

I'm kinda worried about your *priorities*, dude! Most people *want* to do well in school and show up at their brothers' weddings!

I KNOW HE'S RIGHT.

BUT "MOST PEOPLE" AREN'T *AVENGERS*.

Hey-- Cap?

I'm *ready*.

All *this* one has to do is sit in class and say "Present!" when the teacher takes attendance.

I'll get all the notes and homework from you and Nakia and Zoe and catch up when I can.

Present!

Present!

See? Easy peasy!

Easy peasy!

I've created a *monster*. Literally. *Un*-figuratively literally.

What about this one?

This one gets to hang out at the bajillion parties that are going to happen between now and when Aamir gets married.

You don't think your own family is going to notice that you're talking in monosyllables?

It'll be *loud!* There will be a *ton* of people! As long as I show up in photos, no one will notice!

Shaadi mubarakbad!*

Shaadi mubarakbad!*

*Blessed wedding!

THEY THINK I CAN'T HANDLE IT.

Oh. Okay.

THEY DON'T REALIZE HOW MUCH STUFF I'M DEALING WITH *OUTSIDE* OF AVENGING. HOME AND SCHOOL AND EVERYTHING--

I WANT TO BE AN AVENGER. AN *AVENGER.*

NOT SOME SUPER HERO *KID SISTER* WHO CAN'T *CLEAN UP* AFTER HERSELF.

THE NEXT MORNING.

--in conclusion, the system is *rigged.*

Thank you, Leslie. Very informative.

Who's up next? Kamala?

ZZZZZZ

SCHOOL, *AVENGING,* ALMOST BUT NOT QUITE FAILING MATH, AND NOW THERE'S GONNA BE A *WEDDING* AND A WHOLE EXTRA *PERSON* LIVING IN MY HOUSE...

HOW AM I SUPPOSED TO KEEP ALL THIS STRAIGHT IN MY HEAD?

CRUNCH

IT'S LIKE I NEED TO BE IN THREE PLACES AT ONCE JUST TO GET EVERYTHING *DONE.*

Ah crap, it's *her!*

I didn't know they **made** proper, traditional girls like you anymore!

Well done, beta...for once in your life, you haven't made an utter **embarrassment** of yourself...

Can we at least **talk** about this?!

You've got to start thinking about the future, beta... a married man has responsibilities...

What **now?!**

RRRRING RRING!

Hello?

Hey, kid. It's your friendly neighborhood **Iron Man.**

Are you at a **bar** or something? It's really **loud.**

One, I'm **sixteen,** two, I don't drink--

That's great, that's great. Me either. Listen--

Our intel says a classified shipment of **experimental** neurotoxin has been stolen from the Port of Jersey City. That's **your** turf--you know it better than **any** of us.

If you take care of it, Cap'll be putting **gold stars** next to your name on the **team roster** from here to eternity.

You can wear **this** one for the engagement, **this** one for the walima--

Oh my God. Thank you. This is **exactly** the opportunity I've been waiting for--

RRING! RRRING!

Excellent. Hey, how'd your **physics homework** turn out?

Other than the fact that I got **half wrong?** Just fine. Hold on-- my **other** phone is ringing--

And one of the *reasons* I respect you is because you would *never* reject a rishta with a smart, beautiful, honorable woman because of some outdated idea that a good bride looks like a circa-1989 Bollywood commercial for *Fair and Lovely.**

Right?

Right?

I kind of hate this conversation.

* A skin-lightening cream popular in Asia.

Ahem.

Well--

Of course, we didn't mean to *imply* that--

We're not *prejudiced*, Aamir, you know--

It's just that--you're my only son, jaannu.

We're so far away from our families...when I think of your wedding, I think of something *familiar*, with people like us. The right family, the right background--

None of that guarantees a good match, Ammi.

Kamran was *perfect*, and look how *that* turned out.

HEY!

Even if we said yes, how would you *support* yourselves? Where would you live?

Well, we've talked it over, and...I'm willing to live *here* until Aamir finishes his degree, if that helps. Then, once he's set up, we can find our own place.

Wait, *what?!*

Acha! That puts a different spin on the matter.

A new bride in the *family home...* apna maan rakhliye!*

*You have kept alive our traditions.

ONCE UPON A TIME, ON A SUNDAY AFTERNOON...

Ammi, Abu, Kamala...

...there's, uh... there's something we want to discuss with you.

We didn't want to make plans until... I mean, we asked if...

What we mean to say is--

Here's the thing--

We want to get married!

You WHAT?!

YASSS!

Come on. I have no idea what just happened here, but I think you gotta *leave* this for now and live to fight another day.

Rumors *suck*. They never really go away, they just *change shape*...

But--

--I don't understand. I thought everything would go back to normal once I *fixed* things...

Would you literally kill me if I said you're the hero Jersey City deserves?

Yes, I would literally kill you.

WHOMP!

BEING SUPER-FAMOUS IS TURNING OUT COMPLETELY *DIFFERENTLY* FROM WHAT I IMAGINED. WHAT MS. MARVEL *REPRESENTS* HAS GOTTEN WAY BIGGER THAN WHAT I AM.

I NEED *MORE* THAN JUST A CAPE AND A MASK. WHAT I *REALLY* NEED, NOW MORE THAN EVER...

Come on...let's lie low for a while. I've got *cookie dough* waiting in the freezer.

What'd I *miss*, anyway?

...IS *FRIENDS*.

I'll explain later--we've gotta *help* her!

Have you ever tried to discover just how *high* a voltage your unique cellular structure can take before *die-off* begins?

Shall we find out?

S-STOP!

GAAH!

HNNNGH!

You *first*, creepfest!

ZZT ZZZT!

ZZT ZZZT!

Are you okay?!

Y-yeah. *Shaken*, but yeah.

Thanks, Mike. I *owe* you one.

Oh yeah? Ever thought of what you owe the *rest* of us?

No! Stop! Ms. Marvel--

M-Mike-- get Bruno--

Hey! Bruno! Inhale *deeply* through your nose!

Buhh!

Man...what a *migraine*...

Hnngh--

You're okay!

Mike! Hey! What's-- what's going on here?!

FFSST

FSST

FSST!

CARRIE-ANNE MOSS, EAT YOUR HEART OUT.

You'll never get away with this! You can't stand in the way of progr--

WHOMP!

--AAAAH!

THUNK

I didn't come back from the dead for this. You've made an enemy for *life* today, Ms. Marvel!

You're in way over your head!

AACK!

Are you going to be all right?

Yeah. Thanks. I'm *trying* to keep it together, only--

I know. It's hard sometimes. When the people you love best are in trouble, it's like you can't focus.

I'm gonna focus. If Bruno needs my help, I have to.

He must... he must really *trust* you if he's given you the key to all this stuff...all the innermost workings of his weirdo *brain*.

Yeah. I think he does. Only... there are *some* parts of his weirdo brain that I know he *doesn't* want me to see.

There's this *girl*--she's his *best friend*, and apparently he was in love with her for, like, *ever*.

Oh. *Uhh.* That's-- awkward.

Yeah. And she's really sweet and funny and pretty in a totally non-*obnoxious* way. But I think she *hates* me-- she avoids me in the hall at school, she never wants to talk--

Maybe she just needs time to *adjust*. Maybe the whole best-friend-dating-someone-else thing came as a *total shock* and she hasn't really wrapped her mind around it yet.

Maybe. I just wish I didn't feel so... *intimidated*.

We, *umm*... we should get back to work.

You're right, you're right.

Okay, here goes nothing...

Are you sure this is *legal*?

Eeek! That's *loud*!

KABOOM!

Probably not.

But we don't have a minute to lose--the, *uhh,* bad guys have managed to make their mind-controlling nanotech *airborne.* The entire city could be infected tomorrow, and then there'll be no one to stand in their way...

Sorry. I don't exactly have quiet, *pretty* powers.

How long until we know whether Bruno managed to design an antidote?

I'm pulling up the login site now... once we're sitting down, I'll input the encrypted passkey from my *pendant...*

How does a piece of *jewelry* have an encrypted passkey on it, anyway?

It's got a *flash drive* inside. His whole DNA sequence is on there, too. I think he was trying to be *romantic... some* guys write poetry, some give you their *genetic code* on a USB stick...

RIGHT ABOUT THEN, I FIGURE OUT SOMETHING *IMPORTANT:*

I'm sorry, it's just...

I'd lose my mind if something *bad* happened to that nerd...

It's okay. We're gonna fix this. We're gonna *save* him.

SHE *LOVES* HIM. SHE *REALLY* LOVES HIM.

He's been **kidnapped,** and it's all my fault--

Oh. Oh. Oh.

Oh, **no...**

I didn't know you and Bruno were **close.** I mean, everybody's seen you around together a few times, but he always talked about it like it was a **coincidence...**

We're...

We're only as close as we have to be. I'm sorry, I didn't mean to get this upset.

It's fine. If I wasn't completely in **shock,** I'd be bawling too.

What do we do now? My moms are **lawyers**--they could totally raise heck to mobilize the JCPD--

No lawyers. Before he was kidnapped, Bruno said that **you** were the only one who could help.

Me?!

He was working on something in the **science lab**--analyzing some weird purple goop I gave him. He was close to a breakthrough. He said you have the "key to his heart," whatever that means.

Oh, Bruno...

I think... I think I know what he meant.

What?

He syncs all his data to this **private cloud service** run by a bunch of other kid geniuses.

And **I** have the passkey.

--and I've tried his cell, like, four times, but it goes straight to voicemail.

I'm *not* being paranoid. He always calls me after his shift at the Circle Q. I just have this weird feeling that something is--

THUMP!

Huh?!

Michaela Gutierrez Miller?

... I'm gonna have to call you back, Lizzy. Bye-bye.

Oh my flying spaghetti monster. You're *her*. You're *Ms. Marvel*. Ms. Marvel is *in* my *room*--

I have some *questions* to ask you about Bruno Carrelli.

Is he okay? What's going on? He's not answering his phone...

He's-- he's--

PEW! PEW!

Hail Hydra.

Don't do this. You *have* to come with me. I can't fix this without you. Bruno--

BUT THERE'S NO TIME.

IT'S HIM OR ME. HIM OR THE FATE OF OUR *WHOLE CITY*, MAYBE...

SMASH!

SO I LEAVE HIM THERE. MY BEST FRIEND. I LEAVE HIM WITH HYDRA.

AND THE WORST PART?

PEW! PEW!

IF I HAD TO, I WOULD DO IT *AGAIN*.

Want me to take one of the trucks and go after her?

No need, Chuck.

We have something she *wants*... right here.

AAAAH!

ZZZT!

You see? I told you we've been watching you.

We are well aware of your weaknesses.

Thank you for that, Bruno.

I like my new job.

Bruno... no...

New job. Hail Hydra.

As you will soon discover *firsthand!*

FFSST!

Aack!

Nnngh--

Stop making this so hard for yourself, Ms. Marvel.

HYDRA is *unstoppable*... cut off one head, and *two* will grow in its place...

Did you know that nanotech can be dispersed as an *aerosol?* Amazing, really. My men and I have been inoculated against its effects.

The residents of *Jersey City,* on the other hand...

DON'T BREATHE THE WEIRD PURPLE GAS DON'T BREATHE THE WEIRD PURPLE--

Sorry, y'all need to stay down.

Not *again*--

Oof!

You know, I'm getting really tired of this--

I'VE GOT TO GET BRUNO *OUT* OF HERE AND FIGURE OUT HOW TO REVERSE WHATEVER THEY'VE DONE TO HIM--AND TO THE *REST* OF DOWNTOWN JERSEY CITY.

Whooaa!

WHOOSH

Learn to recognize when you're *beaten,* kid!

BZZT!

Funny, I don't *feel* very beaten.

Buuh!

CLONK!

Hnngh!

But *you* look like you're not doing so hot.

OKAY. I CAN DEAL WITH MUTATED COCKATIELS, GIANT ROBOTS, AND NEFARIOUS SCHEMES TO DESTROY MY HOMETOWN.

This young man has a very adept mind. Who would have thought you could find a *boy genius* with an IQ of 170 working at a *Circle Q* in Jersey City?

That was my *old job.* I like my *new job.*

Good lad.

BUT BRAINWASHING MY BEST FRIEND? *THIS* IS WHERE I DRAW THE LINE.

I can't let you do this.

How do you plan to *stop* us?

We've been *watching* you, Ms. Marvel. Your rapid rise to prominence has not gone *unnoticed.*

Is it possible you've risen *too* far, *too* fast? Running with the *Avengers* entails a great deal of... *pressure.* And the public? The public is not always kind. Even to its *heroes.*

You *knew* what would happen when you put my face on that billboard. You've been trying to *discredit* me. It's part of your *plan.*

You were a potential *annoyance.* What other costumed hero would lift a finger to protect this shambling little city?

It was necessary for you to be... *compromised.*

WHERE...

...AM I?

Ah. Ms. Marvel. We've been expecting you for quite some time now.

I've been told you are... *resourceful.* Which is why I thought it best to *wait* for you to come to us.

And now, here you are.

My name is *Dr. Faustus.* Welcome to Hope Yards Development and Relocation Association.

Hope Yards... **D**evelopment and **R**elocation... **A**ssociation.

HYDRA!

Precisely.

Real estate was an obvious move for us...present your plan to dominate an entire city as an *investment opportunity* and no one bats an eye.

The *nanotech beverages* were almost unnecessary... but a nice touch, don't you think?

You.. you're forcing people out of their homes...their businesses...

No one has been *forced* to do anything. We're simply giving the *natural process* of wealth concentration a little *nudge.*

Whoooa!

P-please don't hurt me... I'm just lower-level management...

I'm not gonna hurt anybody. I just need you to take a message to your *bosses.*

Shut down the nanotech, decommission the security drones and leave town. Or there are gonna be *consequences.*

Tell them *yourself.*

We're pulling up to HQ right now. And if you think a couple of *security drones* are bad...

...wait until you see the *big toys.*

GREAT. A GIANT, ABANDONED WAREHOUSE. IF WE WERE IN A MOVIE, THIS IS WHERE I'D DISAPPEAR AND NEVER BEEN HEARD FROM *EVER AGAIN.*

Hnngh!

BOOM!

Night-night time, Ms. Marvel.

AAAAND THAT'S PRETTY MUCH ALL I REMEMBER FOR THE NEXT LITTLE BIT.

SOMETHING TELLS ME I DON'T HAVE MUCH TIME.

Don't fail me now, Bruno...

Bruno? Hey--so we have a new problem.

I just saw Josh and Radislav and a bunch of other people wandering around Hope Yards like *zombies.* Like they'd been *brainwashed* by an *actual* evil overlord.

I'm not surprised.

You're *not?!*

Nope. I made a slide of that purple goop from the mini-fridge and looked at it under the high-powered microscope, and guess what I found--

"--*nanotech.* Anybody who drank that stuff has ingested *thousands* of little artificial viruses. They're being *reprogrammed,* neuron by neuron.

"They're probably crawling all over Josh's *frontal cortex* right this second."

Crap. I'm gonna have to move *fast,* then.

Tell Ms. Norris I won't be in physics class today-- I'm going to see if I can follow one of these Hope Yards *catalog models* back to wherever their corporate headquarters is.

Sounds g-- oh no.

Right, Radislav?

Right. Property values...great for the city...

I don't mind commuting *two hours* to work... I *like* the suburbs... rent's *cheap* there...

AMMI'S WRONG ABOUT THIS ONE.

IF YOU IGNORE YOUR PROBLEMS, THEY DON'T GO AWAY--THEY JUST GET *WORSE*.

I *CAN'T* HANG UP MS. MARVEL'S MASK WHEN THERE'S THIS MUCH AT STAKE.

Sorry, Tyesha-- I'd love to stay and get to know you better, but there's something I *really* gotta do before school starts.

Oh. I--

Kamala, you *promised!*

After school, Aamir! I *promise*- promise!

I don't know what's gotten into her lately. You can't get a word in edgewise anymore.

I was the same way at that age. I bet *you* were too. Let her be.

Let's just... take a walk toward the *masjid*.

Or *anywhere* in the direction of *away*.

Sounds good to me.

--special reason you need to be here, ma'am?

It's a *public sidewalk*. I'm walking on it.

Tyesha! What's going on here? Is there a problem?

No problem, homie! We've just had a couple little break-ins at Hope Yards and we're trying to make sure everybody here is somebody who *needs* to be here.

Did he just call me *homie*?

This is a *city!* People walk through here to go to work and school and stuff!

True. But this used to be a *bad neighborhood*, you know. Our residents expect a high level of *security*.

Residents?

Yup! Hope Yards is filling up!

Everybody has a girlfriend except me!

Stop saying *girlfriend*! Tyesha is *not* my girlfriend! We're doing this properly!

Fine. Okay. I'll be a good *mahram** and chaperone your *non*-date with your *non*-girlfriend.

Good. I was thinking I could walk you to school and we could pick her up along the way--

Lovely.

*A family member with whom one is permitted to be alone in private.

As-salaamu alaykum, sister Tyesha. Yes, she's--uh-huh. Great. Can you meet us at the corner of 12th and Grove?

I cannot *believe* this.

She'll be here in three minutes!

Are you gonna warn her that you *drool* while you sleep? 'Cause that seems like *vital spousal information.*

No, and neither are you!

We're just going to have a nice, mature conversation about our *expectations*--

"...you can't choose to *be* a hero! You can only choose to *do* what a hero would do!"

Another four-hours-of-sleep day. That's three in a row...

Hey! Kamala! Wait up!

You never showed up at the masjid yesterday.

I got sidetracked!

I was waiting for you! There was something I needed to do that I couldn't do without *you!*

What are you talking about?

There's, uh--I needed to talk to somebody. Somebody I can't talk to *alone*. I need another, umm, *girl* there. To *chaperone* us.

Wait a second. You wanted to talk to a *girl*?

Yeah.

You have a *girlfriend*?!

Istaghfirullah! Of course not! She's a girl I'm speaking to *only* with *correct supervision* for the purposes of discussing marriage!

Do you know what time it is? Where have you been?

Out *super-heroing*. We've been *through* all this, Ammi. As long as I keep my *grades* up, you promised not to tell anybody and to let me do my thing--

This time it's *different!* Look at what people are saying about you! You can't *enlargement* your way out of this one, beta!

THE JERSEY JOURNAL

SUPER HERO OR SELLOUT?

Embiggen. It's embiggen, Ammi.

Whatever! I don't want you involved in a public scandal. Ms. Marvel needs to take a rest until all of this is over.

What? No!

What, *yes.* A hero is only a hero when the people are *with* her.

When they turn *against* her, she becomes--

Please don't say "villain."

I was going to say *lafungah.**

*A useless idiot who has failed at life.

And with that, I'm going to bed.

You do so! And remember...

I TELL MYSELF NOT TO TAKE THE THINGS NAKIA SAID *PERSONALLY*.

SHE DOESN'T KNOW IT'S ME. SHE SAW THE GIANT BILLBOARD AND THOUGHT MS. MARVEL DID SOMETHING SHE DIDN'T ACTUALLY DO.

I MEAN...DID SOMETHING *I* DIDN'T ACTUALLY DO.

2nd

GROVE ST

I HAVE TO KEEP IT TOGETHER. THE LINE BETWEEN BEING ON-DUTY AS MS. MARVEL AND BEING OFF-DUTY AS KAMALA KHAN IS GETTING *WOBBLY*.

I'M STARTING TO *SLIP*.

Hello, beta.

Ammi! You scared the cr--the heck out of me!

This can't be happening.

I gotta make this right... *Ms. Marvel* has to get on camera and make some kind of *statement*...

Whoa, wait! Maybe that's what they *want!* We have *no idea* what these Hope Yards people are really about--we need more *data* before we can make a real plan--

Just let me analyze the *purple goop* so we know exactly what we're up against.

Fine. Okay. Can you do it by *tomorrow morning?*

Sure, no problem. I've only got physics homework, math homework, my shift at the Circle Q--

And let's not forget *Mike.*

You should talk to her! You might actually like her! She wants to meet you--

Some other time, Bruno!

I have *bad guys* to fight.

Everything is getting crazy!

Even with all the fancy Avengers combat training I've been doing, I barely got out of there alive!

Is it even *legal* for private security drones to *shoot* at unarmed civilians?

Dude, these days? Legal is what you can *get away with,* not what's in the *law.*

Did you say you found this purple goop in a *mini-fridge?*

Yeah, and there was a bunch more. Like they were giving it out for free or something. Compliments of Hope Yards.

Well, if I take it to the science lab at school, it's possible I could analyze it for--

Hey! It's that protest from earlier!

--a small but growing demonstration, which began earlier today.

The movement has hometown hero Ms. Marvel in its crosshairs for allegedly--

Maybe we should turn this off.

No! I wanna see!

SLAM!

SOMETIMES, EVEN THE BEST SUPER HERO NEEDS TO RETRACE HER STEPS.

FIGURE OUT WHERE SHE WENT *WRONG*.

I must have missed something last time...

There's no way a development corporation with actual security drones has nothing to hide...

LOOK FOR THOSE LITTLE CLUES THAT SAY "YOU SCREWED UP HERE. THERE WILL BE *FALLOUT!*"

BLIP! BLIP! BLIP!

Normal walls, normal Pottery Barn catalogue chairs, normal everything--

What am I looking for?

Normal communal organic kombucha stash--

LITTLE CLUES...

LIVE LOVE KOMBUCHA
LIFE IS A BEACH
#BLESSED
LIVE YOUR TRUTH!

Or, you know, *not*.

What even *is* this stuff?

...BIG CONSEQUENCES.

I kind of hate *shrinking*...

No matter how many times I do it, it never gets less weird to see soda cans the size of *minivans*...

KAMALA? HELLLOOO?

I coulda sworn she went this way...

Huh?!

Just keep walking! Away!

Let's *never* do this again. Tiny Ms. Marvel is *terrifying*.

Fine by me! Since you're already spending 99% of your time with your *non-tiny* girlfriend!

Hey. I know you're *upset*, but that wasn't cool.

Don't be that guy. You're *not* that guy. Mike is *great* the way she is.

Oh, no. They look pretty *mad*, Ms. M.

Yeah. Yeah, they do.

You gonna be *okay* out there?

I really hope so.

What are you gonna do now?

Figure out who's behind this "redevelopment" stuff and *stop* them-- before the *whole city* gets swallowed up!

So why's your picture up there anyway? They giving you some kind of *kickback*?

No! I never agreed to this!

It's like I've become *public property*...

When nobody knew who I was, I could just show up and take care of the bad guys and leave again. But now...

Now I'm some kind of *symbol*, and I don't have any say in what it *means*.

It means you're doing *good things*, and people are *paying attention*.

I guess so.

But how am I gonna *cope* if I can't get *corned beef bahn mi* from the only Serbian-Vietnamese grocery in Jersey City?

You'll survive. We all will. *Somehow.*

Oh, good. I think we lost the swarm of *security drones*.

Tell that to *these* guys...

HE'S NOT WRONG.

I *DO* HAVE A LOT OF PROBLEMS RIGHT NOW...

AND NUMBER ONE IS--

DOOF!

WOOOUH

HOW DO A COUPLE OF STANDARD ISSUE *SECURITY GUARDS* GET THEIR HANDS ON STATE-OF-THE-ART *CROWD DISPERSAL WEAPONS?*

Hnngh!

There! Problem *solved.*

N-not really...

Unnngh...

Phase one, phase two-- They want to build over the entire city.

Come on, guy. You got your check, now move it along--

It's not that simple!

Huh?

You can't just tear down my store and cut me a check! What you paid me wouldn't buy five feet of *sidewalk* in Manhattan! I ran the grocery on this corner for *twenty years!*

You can't... you can't just come into a community and pave it over, and call that... progress...

Cute sermon, guy. Now move it or *lose* it.

Your *"community"* ain't our problem.

He's right. It's *my* problem now.

And if you guys don't give Radislav another three feet of personal space, *you* are gonna be my problem, *too.*

In that case, lady...

I guess you got a *lotta* problems right now.

POUND POUND!

Hello? Anybody in there? I have a *complaint!*

LOCKED--

THIS PLACE IS A GHOST TOWN. HOW DOES SOMETHING THIS BIG AND COMPLICATED GET SLAPPED DOWN OVERNIGHT?

AND WHY AREN'T MORE PEOPLE FREAKING OUT ABOUT IT?

Hnngh!

You're too *sweet*, squishy muffin. You give people *way* too much credit.

Getting out of bed this morning was clearly a mistake.

I've gotta run. I'm supposed to meet my brother at the mosque in like five minutes. See you all later.

Wait, Kamala--

Not now, Bruno.

THAT WASN'T A LIE, BY THE WAY. I *AM* SUPPOSED TO MEET AAMIR AT THE MOSQUE IN FIVE MINUTES.

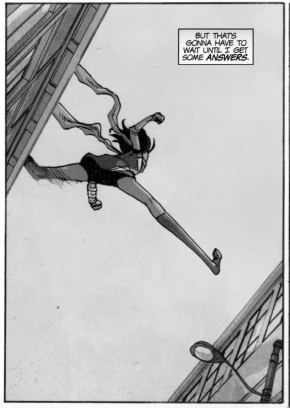

BUT THAT'S GONNA HAVE TO WAIT UNTIL I GET SOME *ANSWERS.*

Hnngh!

THUNK!

"Downtown Revitalization Project"?

Wait! You can't just use a giant picture of somebody without asking their permission first!

Ms. Marvel is an American icon! She belongs to *everybody*!

See you later, kids!

SLAM!

What is happening?!

Don't freak out--there's gotta be some kind of explanation--

What?! No! That's not what's happening here!

Whoa. That's... intense.

Does she really *smile* like that?

This is so *typical*.

Some up-and-coming hero parks herself in a majority-minority neighborhood, makes it *cool*, and then *sells out* to the first bloodsucking developer who wants to tear it all down to make *luxury condos*.

Oh, yeah? Explain what *Ms. Superfamous* is doing up there, in that case.

Maybe she doesn't know! Maybe she's been so busy trying to save the Tristate Area from *intergalactic threats* that she's sort of accidentally let a bunch of things slide!

Did you sign some kind of weird *product endorsement* or something?

No! I've never seen this before!

Hi there! Here to take a look at one of our *model units*?

Uhh... what?

What is this place? What did you do to all the stuff that was here yesterday? Where's *Radislav's Grocery*? Why am--what is Ms. Marvel doing on that billboard up there?

YOU CAN...
EAN UP JERSEY CITY!
[...] / RELOCATION ASSOCIATION

Amazing, isn't she? Such an *inspiration*. So great to see someone like her making Jersey City into a better place.

UMAMAMI SUSHI

A better place for *people*, not for artisanal sushi restaurants!

Hey, people need to eat! Let them eat *sushi!* Haha!

That was a little joke.

Here, take a couple of these. My name is Chuck. I'm happy to answer any questions you might have.

On behalf of *Hope Yards Development,* thanks for visiting Phase I of our downtown Revitalization Project.

I just didn't expect it to happen so *soon*.

I never meant to hurt you. I've *tried* to talk to you about Mike, but you're so busy being an *Avenger* that you're never around anymore.

Are you being *safe*? I mean, you know-- taking precautions?

What?! Whoa. Hey.

I am *so* not prepared to have this conversation with you!

COMICS R GAMES

FOY'S COMICS

But since you asked, of *course* we're being...

...safe.

That's it for today, folks. Test prep tomorrow--

And *no*, you can't short-circuit the *lightning golems* for extra credit. Leave those poor things alone.

Hey--

WHOOP! WHOOP!

Can we at least *talk* about this?

What's there to talk about?

You told me you were *in love* with me, then I see you *kissing* some random girl in the hallway.

Because you told me it wasn't gonna work between us!

"I've gotta focus on my *dream*, Bruno, don't wait for me, Bruno, live your life, Bruno--"

It's been *eight months*.

You said I should try to be happy *without* you. So that's what I'm doing. I'm *trying*.

I--I know.

Mike is a *girl.*

Short for *Michaela,* apparently.

When did this happen?

Like six weeks ago! Where have *you* been?

Are they... *together?*

Uhh, *yes?*

But they're not, like, *together-* together, right?

I mean... biblically together?

Yeah, hon.

"I think they probably are."

I JUST THINK OF THAT MOMENT BRUNO AND I HAD ON THE ROOF. IT WAS PRETTY MUCH YESTERDAY, OR AT LEAST, THAT'S HOW IT FEELS.

AND MY BRAIN JUST SHUTS DOWN.

Hey!

I gotta get to class.

AND SUDDENLY I START TO THINK...

THINGS HAVE CHANGED AT SCHOOL TOO.

ALL THE BITS THAT WERE DESTROYED BY THE INVENTOR'S MINIONS HAVE BEEN *REBUILT*, AND THANKS TO A GRANT FROM *STARK INDUSTRIES*, WE HAVE, LIKE, ALL THIS NEW STUFF IN THE SCIENCE LAB.

PLUS LOKI'S LIGHTNING GOLEMS. I GUESS THEY *LIKE* US OR SOMETHING, OR MAYBE THEY WERE JUST *TOO DUMB* TO EVER LEAVE.

EVEN *ZOE ZIMMER* IS DIFFERENT NOW. THAT WHOLE THING WITH THE WORLD ALMOST ENDING GAVE HER SOME KIND OF *EXISTENTIAL CRISIS*, AND NOW SHE'S GOING THROUGH THIS WHAT-DOES-IT-ALL-MEAN PHASE.

Morning, sleepyhead! Zoe brought caffeine!

Are you going to gym class? I'm thinking of coming down with *sudden flu-like symptoms*...

Buhh...

WHAT CAN I SAY? IT'S LIKE WE'RE ALL *GROWING UP*.

Where's Bruno? I have his physics notes.

He's with Mike. Like always.

Who's Mike?

What do you mean, "Who's Mike?"

Have you been on autopilot for the last month and a half?

What? What are you talking about? Who is this Mike person? What *secret bromance* am I missing here?

DON'T GET ME WRONG, IT'S BEEN A LOT OF HARD WORK.

THE LEARNING CURVE IS STEEP. I'VE HAD TO BE FASTER, STRONGER, SMARTER--

GROVE STREET, JERSEY CITY.
Post Rat-villain Obliteration.

--AND STILL BE HOME BY CURFEW.

Later, kid!

Iron Man! You're leaving?! You were supposed to help me with my *physics* homework!

Hey, hey--when I'm wearing my Nikes, it's *Tony.*

I've got a date! Just round everything to the *nearest decimal point* and you'll be fine!

SCHOOL, AVENGERS, MY REGULAR BI-WEEKLY DUNGEON GROUP IN *ANCIENT SCROLLS ONLINE...*

IT'S ALL GREAT, BUT IT'S WHAT ABU WOULD CALL A *PROBLEM OF PLENTY.*

AND THE THING ABOUT A PROBLEM OF PLENTY IS...

ZZZZZZ...

IT'S STILL A *PROBLEM.*

MS. MARVEL
ARMY OF ONE

writer **G. WILLOW WILSON**

Ms. Marvel #1-3, #8-11
artists **TAKESHI MIYAZAWA**
WITH **ADRIAN ALPHONA** (#1, PP. 22-30; #8-11, FLASHBACKS)

Ms. Marvel #5-6
artist **NICO LEON**

Ms. Marvel #7
artist **ADRIAN ALPHONA**

Ms. Marvel #12
artist **MIRKA ANDOLFO**

color artists **IAN HERRING** WITH **IRMA KNIIVILA** (#8)
letterer **VC'S JOE CARAMAGNA**
cover art **CLIFF CHIANG** (#1-3),
DAVID LOPEZ (#4-6) & **CAMERON STEWART** (#7-12)

assistant editor
CHARLES BEACHAM

editor
SANA AMANAT

collection editor JENNIFER GRÜNWALD
assistant editor DANIEL KIRCHHOFFER
assistant managing editor MAIA LOY
assistant managing editor LISA MONTALBANO

vp production & special projects JEFF YOUNGQUIST
svp print, sales & marketing DAVID GABRIEL
vp licensed publishing SVEN LARSEN
editor in chief C.B. CEBULSKI